Enjoy the tour of our beautiful city !

Pamela Bove

and

MaryCarol Berchman

Chicago's The Place

Written by The Mrs. "B"s
MaryCarol Berchman
and
Pamela Bove
Mother and daughter co-authors

Illustrated by
Kathy O'Malley

Elameno P Publishing
CHICAGO, IL

ISBN: 978-0-615-60248-6
Library of Congress Catalog Control Number 2014930540

Elameno P Publishing

CHICAGO, IL 60616

Printed by MCRL

Printed in China

**To Our Grandparents, Children and Grandchildren
Now is the time to create treasured memories**

MaryCarol & Pamela

**For everyone who loves
Chicago — the place
where all my dreams have come true.**

with tremendous gratitude ~ Kathy

"Pick me, Pick me," shrieked Lily,
As she wildly waved her hand.
"Show and Tell is my favorite,
Please, please me, Mrs. McMann."

I can't believe she pointed,
Directly right at me.
I felt my freckles beaming.
"Come up Lily, 1...2...3."

I exploded from my classroom chair,
My curls danced around my face.
I visited Grandma this summer,
And WOW, Chicago's The Place!

To share my summer adventure,
I have made a scrapbook for you.
It highlights all the attractions,
There was so much for us to do.

Come along with me on my trip,
You'll just love how my story ends.
My Grandma gave me a surprise,
To share with my whole class of friends.

Millennium Park was on Monday,
We played beneath the shiny bean.
Grandma's reflection kept changing,
From tall to short to lean.

We frolicked in famed Crown Fountain,
Splashing water at each other.
I wish our pictures were up there,
Silly faces one after another.

Tuesday was a day of fashion,
We shopped the Magnificent Mile.
Buying shoes and a shiny pink purse,
We left Michigan Avenue in style.

Colorful Buckingham Fountain,
Was a spectacular light display.
The water shot high in the sky,
A perfect ending to our day!

Grandma woke me on Wednesday,
"Get up Lily, it's time to go!
We have to get to the ballpark,
Before we miss the first throw."

We cheered for the talented White Sox,
Munching peanuts on the Southside.
Singing "Take Me Out to the Ball Game,"
Extra innings the game was all tied.

We then headed to the Northside,
Because Chicago has two clubs.
Their home is classic Wrigley Field,
The blue and red Chicago Cubs.

Both Chicago baseball teams,
Have many devoted fans.
My Grandma, she likes the Cubs,
And me I just wave my hands.

Gram and I make a great team,
We both laugh and sing and clap.
But most of all I love her,
When I sit upon her lap.

Fishing in Burnham Harbor,
With Soldier Field in plain view,
Just me and Grandma side by side,
In Thursday's morning dew.

We headed to Willis Tower,
You might know it as the Sears.
It's the tallest in Chicago,
And not as scary as it appears.

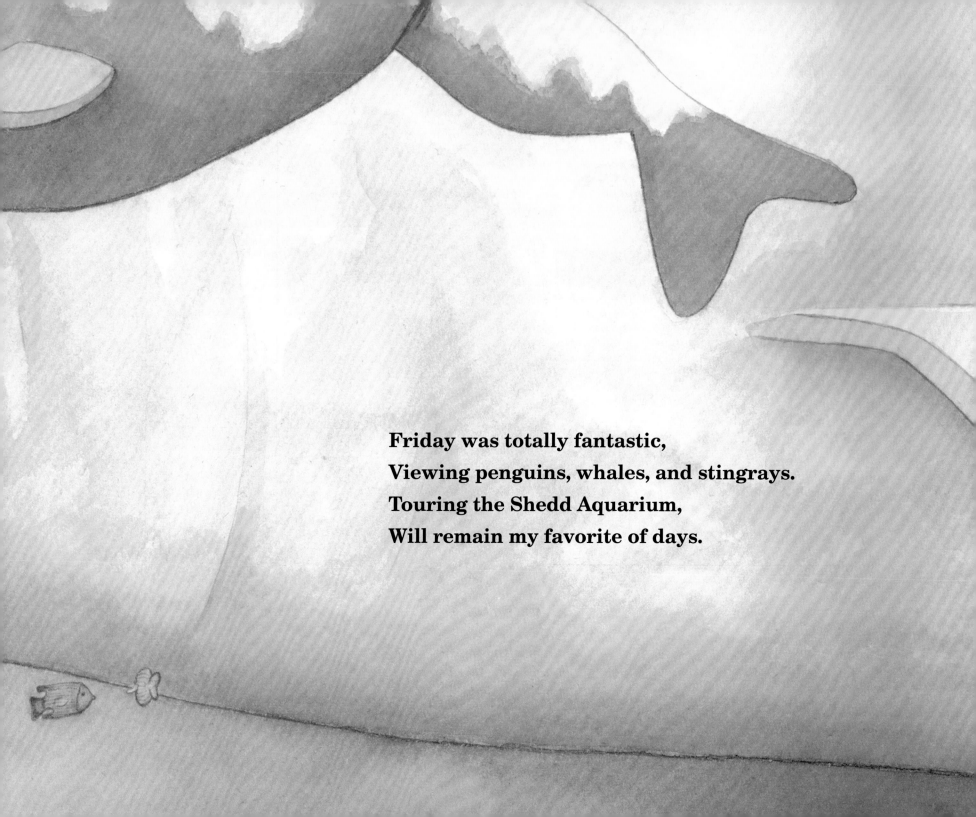

Friday was totally fantastic,
Viewing penguins, whales, and stingrays.
Touring the Shedd Aquarium,
Will remain my favorite of days.

Waking up on Saturday,
Rays of sun were beaming bright.
One more day of vacation,
Just one more magical sight.

Arriving at Navy Pier,
I couldn't believe my eyes.
This is a lakefront playground,
This place really takes the prize!

Merrily sprinting through Pier Park,
Holding on to Grandma's hand,
We arrived at the colorful carousel,
Blaring music of a calliope band.

As we zigzagged through rows of ponies,
Each one galloped and reared with a smile.
I hopped on the whimsical unicorn,
While Grandma rode side-saddle in style!

Waving goodbye to our stallions,
We scurried to join the long line.
The giant, glowing Ferris wheel,
Tickled us to the spine.

As we buckled up for adventure,
The wheel lurched and rose high toward the clouds.
The view was utterly breathtaking,
The skyscrapers, the sailboats, the crowds.

All the sights and sounds made us hungry,
Our tummies growled with a loud roaring voice.
"Only one thing's for dinner," sang Grandma,
"In Chicago deep dish pizza's the choice!"

The buttery crust was incredible,
The tangy tomatoes had real zest.
The gooey cheese stretched for miles,
This pizza was hands down the best!

Grandma had one last highlight for me,
She's so clever at making me smile.
She spread a soft blanket on the ground,
"Lily, come and lay here for a while."

As we gazed toward the star-studded sky,
It burst open with dazzling light.
A rainbow of glittering fireworks,
Created an extravagant sight.

"I'm really lucky to be here," I said,
As I hugged Gram tightly and sighed.
"You have no idea," she echoed,
As we snuggled up alongside.

We hugged goodbye on Sunday,
I gave Grandma a great big kiss.
I love my silly Grandma,
And her laughter I will miss.

id on Summer Vacation ✓

Schedule
8:30am Music
9:00am Vacation
Projects
10:00am Centers
11:00am Recess

Bob   Tim

Scarlet   Elisie   Hurley

When I opened up my suitcase,
There was Grandma's surprise inside.
It's caramel corn from Chicago,
It's the best – try it and decide.

"What an entertaining scrapbook,
And a scrumptious Chicago treat!
Give her a hand!" cheered Mrs. McMann,
"Today's Show and Tell was so sweet."

THE END

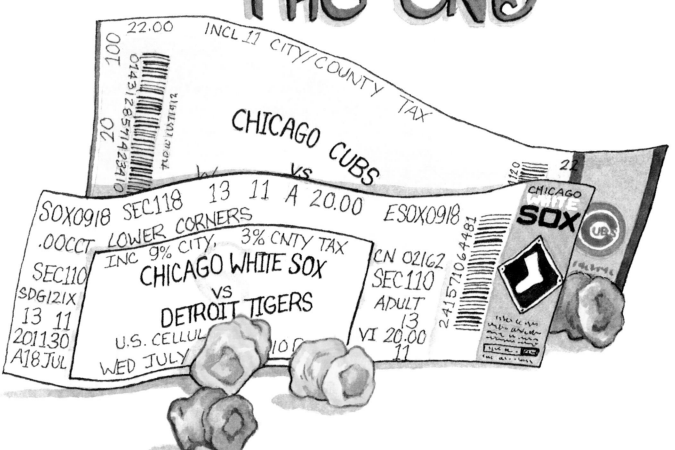